For Timmy, Ma, and Essie xxx
—S. B.

Copyright © 2014 by Suzanne Barton
All rights reserved. No part of this book may be reproduced or transmitted in any form or by any means, electronic or mechanical,
including photocopying, recording, or by any information storage and retrieval system, without permission in writing from the publisher.

First published as *The Dawn Chorus* in Great Britain in April 2014 by Bloomsbury Publishing Plc
Published in the United States of America in February 2016 by Bloomsbury Children's Books
www.bloomsbury.com

Bloomsbury is a registered trademark of Bloomsbury Publishing Plc

For information about permission to reproduce selections from this book, write to
Permissions, Bloomsbury Children's Books, 1385 Broadway, New York, New York 10018
Bloomsbury books may be purchased for business or promotional use. For information on bulk purchases
please contact Macmillan Corporate and Premium Sales Department at specialmarkets@macmillan.com

Library of Congress Cataloging-in-Publication Data
available upon request
ISBN 978-0-8027-3648-2 (hardcover)

Art created with mixed media
Typeset in Lomba Book
Book design by Kayt Bochenski

Printed in China by C&C Offset Printing Co., Ltd., Shenzhen, Guangdong
2 4 6 8 10 9 7 5 3 1

All papers used by Bloomsbury Publishing, Inc., are natural, recyclable products made from wood grown in well-managed forests.
The manufacturing processes conform to the environmental regulations of the country of origin.

The Sleepy Songbird

Suzanne Barton

BLOOMSBURY

NEW YORK   LONDON   OXFORD   NEW DELHI   SYDNEY

Deep in the forest, the trees rustled and the animals stirred. The day had just begun.

Perched on his branch, Peep woke
to the sound of a beautiful song.
"Who's that singing?" he wondered.

Peep stretched out his wings,
fluffed up his feathers . . .

and decided to follow the tune.

He soared on the breeze to the
edge of the forest, where, high
up in a tree, he found an owl.

"Is it you who is singing?" asked Peep.

"It's not me," hooted the owl.

So Peep glided down to the field below, weaving through the grain. And soon he spotted a mouse.

"Is that your wonderful song?" said Peep.

"Not mine," squeaked the mouse.

Peep hopped through the poppies and followed
the song down to the riverbank. As he watched
the water sparkle and swirl, up popped a frog.

"Have you been singing?"
said Peep.

"No!" croaked the frog. "The song
is coming from over there . . ."

Peep looked up and saw an enormous tree on the top of a hill. The tree was full of birds, and they were all singing! Peep landed on one of the branches and listened.

"That was beautiful!" said Peep when they had finished. "I've never heard anything so lovely."

"Thank you!" chirped a friendly bird.
"We're the Dawn Chorus."

"What's the Dawn Chorus?" Peep asked.

"We sing together each morning," said the bird.
"Our song lets everyone know that it's the
start of a new day."

Peep thought for a moment.
"Can I sing with you? Please?"

"Come for an audition tomorrow,"
said the conductor. "We start at dawn."

Peep was so excited that he
flew straight home . . .

and practiced all evening.

And when he couldn't sing
another note, he fell fast asleep.

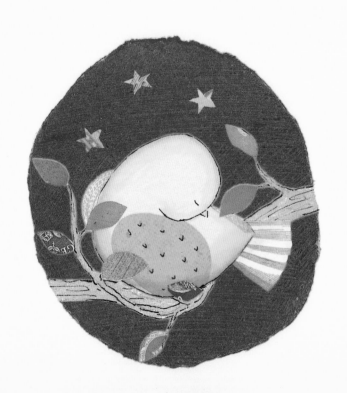

The next morning he awoke in a panic.

"You're going to be late for your audition!" called Owl.

Peep blinked his sleepy eyes in the bright sunshine.

"Oh no!" he cried, and he flew off as fast as he could.

But he was too late.

"I'm sorry, Peep. The day has begun
and the Dawn Chorus has already sung,"
said the conductor.

"Can I have one more chance?"
begged Peep.

"Come back tomorrow," said the conductor. "But don't be late!"

That day, Peep practiced and practiced.
He sang so sweetly that all of the forest
animals stopped to listen.

The hours passed and Peep felt very tired,
but he wouldn't go to sleep—he didn't
want to miss his audition again.

He watched the
stars as night fell.

Just before dawn, Peep set off for the audition. But when he got there, he was so tired that all he could do was . . .

YAWN!

"Oh dear, Peep," the conductor sighed.
"Perhaps you're just not meant to sing with us."

Peep felt very sad as he walked away.
"Now I'll never be part of the Dawn
Chorus," he said to himself.

He flew home all alone. And as the sun started to set, he sang softly.

After a while, Peep heard another sweet song drifting toward him. Not far away, he saw a bird who looked just like him.

"Why can I sing in the evening," asked Peep,
"but not in the morning with the Dawn Chorus?"

"Because you're a nightingale, just
like me," said the bird. "Nightingales
don't sing at dawn, they sing at night!"

So, as the stars came out and the moon shone brightly, the two nightingales sang the most beautiful song of all.